Home on the Range

COWBOY · POETRY

selected by **Paul B. Janeczko**   pictures by **Bernie Fuchs**

DIAL BOOKS NEW YORK

For Dick Abrahamson—my guardian angel, my mentor, my friend P. B. J.

For Harvey B. F.

Published by Dial Books
A Division of Penguin Books USA Inc.
375 Hudson Street, New York, New York 10014
Compilation copyright © 1997 by Paul B. Janeczko
Pictures copyright © 1997 by Bernie Fuchs
All rights reserved • Typography by Atha Tehon with Karen Robbins
Printed in the U.S.A. on acid-free paper
First Edition
1 3 5 7 9 10 8 6 4 2

Library of Congress Cataloging in Publication Data
Home on the range: cowboy poetry / selected by Paul B. Janeczko;
pictures by Bernie Fuchs.—1st ed.
p.   cm.
Summary: Nineteen poems celebrate cowboy life.
ISBN 0-8037-1910-8 (trade).—ISBN 0-8037-1911-6 (lib. bdg.)
1. Cowboys—West (U.S.)—Juvenile poetry. 2. Ranch life—West (U.S.)—Juvenile poetry.
3. Children's poetry, American—West (U.S.) [1. Cowboys—Poetry. 2. Ranch life—Poetry.
3. American poetry—Collections.] I. Janeczko, Paul B. II. Fuchs, Bernie, ill.
PS595.C6H66 1997 811.008'03278—dc20 96-43111 CIP AC

The illustrations were created with pencil and oils on colored paper.

Acknowledgments

Hats Off to the Cowboy © 1989 by Texas Red Songs. / *Definition* and *Old Vogal* from *Write 'Em Cowboy!* © 1993 by Peggy Godfrey.
Originally published by Elliott Publishing. / *You Probably Know This Guy* from *Legacy of the Land* © 1993 by Virginia Bennett.
Originally published by Maverick Publications. / *The Barn Cats* and *Sold Out* from *The Trouble with Dreams* © 1990 by Vess Quinlan.
Originally published by Wind Vein Press. / *Message in the Wind* © 1986 by Jesse Smith. Originally published in *Dealer, Three Wheeler and
the Holstein Steer.* / *A Rare Find* © 1991 by Randall Rieman. / *Rain on the Range* by S. Omar Barker appeared in *Rawhide Rhymes*, published
by Doubleday & Co., 1968. / *Letter from San Pedro* from *No Roof But Sky* © 1990 by Jane Candia Coleman. Originally published by
High Plains Press. / *King of the World* © 1991 by Campfire Echoes. / *Hayin'* from *Granny Tales* © 1989 by Afton Bloxham. Originally published
by AGB Press. / *Cowboy's Favorite* © 1971 by Barney Nelson. / *To Be a Top Hand* from *Just Thinkin* © 1985 by Georgie Sicking. / *Riding
the Wind* from *Pastures Ponies & Pals* © 1993 by Anne Slade and Doris Bircham. / *Range Cow in Winter* © 1986 by Vern C. Mortensen,
and published in *Tumbleweeds and Corral Dust*, a collection of the author's poetry. / *The Trail of an Old Timer's Memory* from
Corral Dust © 1934 by Robert Fletcher.

Table of Contents

Home on the Range · by Brewster Higley 5

Hats Off to the Cowboy · by Red Steagall 6

Definition · by Peggy Godfrey 7

You Probably Know This Guy · by Virginia Bennett 8

The Barn Cats · by Vess Quinlan 10

Message in the Wind · by Jesse Smith 12

A Rare Find · by Randall Rieman 14

Old Vogal · by Peggy Godfrey 16

To the Coyote · by Frank Linderman 18

Rain on the Range · by S. Omar Barker 21

Letter from San Pedro · by Jane Candia Coleman 23

King of the World · by Keith Avery 24

Hayin' · by Afton Bloxham 26

Cowboy's Favorite · by Barney Nelson 28

To Be a Top Hand · by Georgie Sicking 30

Riding the Wind · by Doris Bircham 33

Sold Out · by Vess Quinlan 34

Range Cow in Winter · by Vern Mortensen 37

The Trail of an Old Timer's Memory · by Robert Fletcher 38

Home on the Range

Oh! give me a home where the Buffalo roam,
Where the Deer and the Antelope play;
Where never is heard a discouraging word,
And the sky is not clouded all day.

Brewster Higley

Hats Off to the Cowboy

The city folks think that it's over.
The cowboy has outlived his time—
An old worn-out relic, a thing of the past,
But the truth is, he's still in his prime.

The cowboy's the image of freedom,
The hard-ridin' boss of the range.
His trade is a fair one, he fights for what's right,
And his ethics aren't subject to change.

He still tips his hat to the ladies,
Let's you water first at the pond.
He believes a day's pay is worth a day's work,
And his handshake and word are his bond.

Red Steagall

Definition

I'm not opposed to Western wear
And this may sound absurd
If ya wear the store
But don't punch cattle
Then "cowboy" is just a word.

Peggy Godfrey

You Probably Know This Guy

He gets up in the mornin', way before dawn,
Feeds the wood heater, turns a pot of coffee on,
Tunes in the radio for the market report.
He could stay in bed, but he's just not that sort.

He scrambles some eggs, while his family sleeps upstairs.
Thinks over coffee 'til first light appears.
He climbs into his coveralls when it's light enough to feed.
Some folks wait 'til it's warmer, but he's not of that breed.

The snow crunches as he walks, his breath rises in the cold air.
Tiny icicles begin to form on his moustache hair.
The cows beckon softly, the horses toss their heads and nicker
And stamp their impatience when the tack room lights flicker.

While most folks are asleep, he's out there loadin' up hay.
He could do it blindfolded, since he does it twice every day.
He pauses to stroke a barn cat, and listen to it purr,
Tossles the ears of his cowdog, and pulls out a burr.

Last year's calves chew their alfalfa as the rancher waters.
He's proud of his cows that produced these sons and daughters.
He checks for bad eyes and cows that are due.
This herd needs him badly, and he needs them, too.

He does this every day, every winter, every year,
But it's never monotonous, routine, boring or drear.
To the rest of the world, those are just cows out by the shed
But to this honest cowboy, they're his reason for gettin' out of bed.

Virginia Bennett

The Barn Cats

It's funny, the things you remember;
Like accepting without question
That it was your solemn duty
To study hard and earn big money
Because parents suffered the Depression.

How on your tenth birthday
You walked down to milk
With a staggering headache,
Sat on the one-legged stool
And pressed your forehead
Against her silken flank.

How you remember dull ringing sounds
As the first squirts hit bottom;
How the sound changed to a quiet hiss
As foaming milk filled the shiny bucket;
How the smell of fresh warm milk
Rose to mingle with the clean-cow smell;
How the barn cats sat half-circled,
Mewing politely, insisting there was enough
To fill their little pan.

How the gentle cow responded
To strong brown hands
And let down her milk;
How calmness and forbearance
Were transmitted through your skull;
How your pain was drawn
Into the patient cow.

And now, years later,
You stare out a city window
And ask yourself if big money
Is really better than barn cats
And cow-cured headaches.

Vess Quinlan

Message in the Wind

As you set and look from the ridge,
    To the valley of green down below,
You reach up and pull down yer lid,
    As a cool wind starts to blow.

Yer old pony's eyes are a-lookin',
    His ears workin' forward and back.
All of a sudden you feel his hide tighten,
    And a little hump come into his back.

That hoss's a-readin' a message,
    That's been sent to him in the breeze.
You feel yer gut start to tighten,
    And a shakin' come into yer knees.

Ya look to the right and see nothin',
    Ya look to the left, it's the same.
Except for the birds, rabbits, and squirrels,
    And two hawks a-playin' a game.

But you know yer old hoss ain't a-lying,
    He's as good'ne as you'll ever find.
And you know that old pony's tryin'
    To warn ya 'bout somethin' in time.

Well, ya look real hard where he's lookin',
    His eyes are plumb fixed in a stare,
Then ya see what he's seein',
    A cub and an old mama bear.

The trail you'd a took went between them,
    That old mama bear'd a got tough.
That old pony like as not saved yer hide,
    Or a life shortenin' scare, shor-a-nuff.

You watch 'em go 'cross the meadow,
    And ya ride on yer way once again,
And ya shor thank the Lord for the message,
    He sent to yer hoss on the wind.

Jesse Smith

A Rare Find

It's a wonderful thing,
Though it's hard to explain,
When you meet a new friend on your way,
And you know, in no time,
There's a reason behind
The ease that your friendship's obtained;
For your spirits are one,
Though your friendship's begun
Only just a few hours ago;
Yet the things that you share
And the feelin' that's there
Is more lasting and precious than gold.

Well, your talk ran from cattle
To horses, to shoeing,
To starting these colts a new way.
And before your own eyes
The time has flown by;
Adios is the thing you now say.
But you sure hate to go,
And your feelin's, they show
On your face as you shake your friend's hand.
Still, you know that you're lucky
To have this new friend
Who shares your same love for the land,
For horses and cattle,
For life in the saddle
And nights underneath a clear sky.
A sameness in spirit that goes beyond words—
We share that, my new friend and I.

As I lift up my head
From my old canvas bed,
I thank the good Lord for His care
And for my new friend,
May we soon meet again,
For I know we have much more to share.
See, our spirits are one,
Though our friendship's begun
Only just a few hours ago.
Still, the things that we share
And the feelin' that's there
Is more lasting and precious than gold.

Randall Rieman

Old Vogal

Told me I was lucky
When I went to cut his hay
A bloom or two means lots of leaves
'Course it's best that way.

He assured me I was lucky
That my bales were done up tight
Lucky that I caught the dew
And chanced to bale it right.

Oh yes, and I was lucky
When storm clouds came around
All my hay was in a stack
Not layin' on the ground.

I clenched my jaw and held my tongue
Red anger 'round me swirled
If I was a man, he'd say I was good,
But "lucky" 'cuz I'm a girl.

Peggy Godfrey

To the Coyote

I uster hate ye once, but now
I've weakened some, an' wonder how
Ye live on airth that's ditched an' fenced,
An' lately, somehow, I've commenced
To like ye.

I uster think ye devil's spawn,
But dang it, all my hate is gone.
I watch ye prowl an' win yer bets
Agin the traps a nester sets
To ketch ye.

Once I practised ornery traits,
An' tempted ye with p'isoned baits;
But if ye'd trust me, an' forgit,
I'd make the play all even yit,
An' feed ye.

It took a time for me to see
What's gittin' you has *landed* me:
Yer tribe, like mine, is gittin' few,
So let's forgit; an' here's to you,
Ol' timer.

If I could, I'd turn the days
Back to wilder border ways;
Then we'd make our treaty strong,
An' try our best to git along,
Dog-gone ye!

Frank Linderman

Rain on the Range

When your boots are full of water and your hat brim's
    all a-drip,
And the rain makes little rivers dribblin' down your
    horse's hip,
When every step your pony takes, it purt near bogs him down,
It's then you git to thinkin' of them boys that work in town.
They're maybe sellin' ribbon, or they're maybe slingin' hash,
But they've got a roof above 'em when the thunder
    starts to crash.
They do their little doin's, be their wages low or high,
But let it rain till hell's a pond, they're always warm and dry.
Their beds are stuffed with feathers, or at worst with
    plenty straw,
While your ol' soggy soogans may go floatin' down the draw.
They've got no rope to fret about that kinks up when it's wet;
There ain't no puddle formin' in the saddle where they set.
There's womenfolks to cook 'em up the chuck they
    most admire
While you gnaw cold, hard biscuits 'cause the cook can't
    build a fire.

When you're ridin' on the cattle range and hit a rainy spell,
Your whiskers git plumb mossy, and you note a mildewed smell
On everything from leather to the makin's in your sack;
And you git the chilly quivers from the water down your back.
You couldn't pull your boots off if you hitched 'em to a mule;
You think about them ribbon clerks, and call yourself a fool
For ever punchin' cattle with a horse between your knees,
Instead of sellin' ribbons and a-takin' of your ease.
You sure do git to ponderin' about them jobs in town,
Where slickers ain't a-drippin' when the rain comes
    sluicin' down.
It's misery in your gizzard, and you sure do aim to quit,
And take most any sheltered job you figger you can git.
But when you've got your neck all bowed to quit
    without a doubt,
The rain just beats you to it, and the sun comes bustin' out!
Your wet clothes start to steamin', and most everywhere
    you pass
You notice how that week of rain has livened up the grass.
That's how it is with cowboys when a rainy spell is hit:
They hang on till it's over—then there ain't no need to quit!

S. Omar Barker

Letter from San Pedro

You write that the leaves
   are falling,
that you stand at your window
   and watch them
scarlet and orange,
caught by the wind.

Here there are no leaves,
   only grass to the edges of sky,
and it is lovely as animals,
   silver, dun, old gold.

When I open my door,
whole fields arch their backs,
run under my feet
without bit or bridle,
   knowing no master
     at all.

Jane Candia Coleman

King of the World

The discussion proceeds
   On just where one stands—
For the rodeo cowboys
   Or the common cowhands.
The opinions continue
   And the debate never fails
'Til we finally realize
   They ride different trails.
One seeks the glamour
   And the glory-filled scene—
The other stays home
   Where things are serene.
Mountains and meadows
   Streams, trees, and sky
My soul oft' soars higher
   Than eagles can fly.
So pursue your great contests
   Of daring-do feats—
Your exploits are needed
   By the fans in the seats—
And savor those moments
   Of applause earning bows,
I'll just stay home
   And keep punching cows.
You may think it's lonely
   Where my cow ponies trod.
But my life's rewarding
   Where it's just me and God.
Find those far-flung arenas
   With their banners unfurled
While you're King of the Cowboys
   I'm King of the World.

Keith Avery

Hayin'

Hayin' season. What a pain!
Two whole months you pray for rain,
But it's dry as it can be.
Not one drop of rain you see—
Until you get the first field mowed.
Then clouds move in and drop their load.

Hayhands, anxious, watch the sky,
Seein' unpaid hours go by.
Sun comes out and there's a breeze.
Moods improve, ulcers ease.
Swathers, balers head out soon.
Some of them break down by noon.

Shear bolts bust off one by one,
Rollers jam, gears won't run.
Knotters quit—they just won't tie.
When they're fixed the hay's too dry!
Bale at night when there's some dew,
Neck is stiff, back aches too.
Hired help is hard to please,
One hates carrots, one hates peas.

One says chicken's all he'll eat,
One devours all that's sweet.
Mercury rises—day by day.
Temperatures and tempers lay
One degree away from blow.
It's getting done—but, oh, so slow!

It's toil and struggle, strain and sweat
To keep things runnin' right—and yet,
Time will come when all we hear
Is how the hay got done—this year!
                              Afton Bloxham

Cowboy's Favorite

When a man spends his life on horseback,
And the country's been his home,
There are things he learns to love
As across the range he roams.

There's the scent of burning cedar
And the rhythmic windmill creak,
The song of a friendly mockingbird,
And sunshine on his cheek.

There's the smell of boiling coffee
Or a lonely coyote call,
The smell of sweaty horseflesh
And a lost calf's mournful bawl.

The light from a kerosene lamp
And the early flow'rs in spring,
These are but a few of
A cowboy's favorite things.

But there's one thing that the cowboy
Loves more than all the rest,
That makes him glad to be alive
And puts strength in his breast.

It's not the song that a fiddle plays
Or the money in his jeans.
It's not a brand new pair o' boots
Or a pot of pinto beans.

It's the promise from the Foreman,
Who rules the Range on High,
That the cows will once more fatten
And that the short grass will not die.

This smell that every cowboy loves,
No matter what the season,
And this sound that chases frowns away
No matter what the reason,

Is a simple thing that fills his heart
With peace from crib to cane,
The gift that brings life to his home,
The sound and smell of rain.

Barney Nelson

To Be a Top Hand

When I was a kid and doing my best to
Learn the ways of our land,
I thought mistakes were never made by
A real top hand.

He never got into a storm with a horse,
He always knew
How a horse would react in any case
And just what to do.

He never let a cow outfigure him
And never missed a loop.
He always kept cattle under control
Like chickens in a coop.

He was never in the right place at the wrong
Time or in anybody's way.
For working cattle he just naturally knew
When to move and when to stay.

I just about broke my neck tryin'
To be and do
All those things a good cowboy just
Naturally knew.

One day while riding with a cowboy
I knew was one of the best,
For he had worked in that country for a long
Time, had taken and passed the test,

I was telling of my troubles, some
Bad mistakes I'd made,
That my dreams of being a top cowgirl
Were startin' to fade.

This cowboy looked at me and said
With a sort of smile,
"A sorry hand is in the way all the time,
A good one just once in awhile."

Since that day I've handled lots of cattle
And ridden many a mile,
And I figure I'm doin' my share if I get
In the way just once in awhile.

Georgie Sicking

Riding the Wind

I am going to ride the wind
when it's blowing hard and strong.
I'll jump on its back
and we'll follow a track
where clouds go loping along.

I am going to ride the wind
when it chases behind the rain,
and whenever it snows
I'll be saddled to go
I'll mount up and grab hold of the reins.

I am going to ride the wind
when it turns to a warm chinook.
We'll spur to the moon,
whistle springtime tunes
and melt icicles in every nook.

I am going to ride the wind
when it whispers to waving grass.
We'll call out to the creek,
sing flowers to sleep
and whinny "Good Night" as we pass.

Doris Bircham

Sold Out

The worst will come tomorrow
When we load the saddle horses.
We are past turning back;
The horses must be sold.

The old man turns away, hurting,
As the last cow is loaded.
I hunt words to ease his pain
But there is nothing to say.

He walks away to lean
On a top rail of the corral
And look across the calving pasture
Toward the willow grown creek.

I follow,
Absently mimicking his walk,
And stand a post away.
We don't speak of causes or reasons.

Don't speak at all;
We just stand there,
Leaning on the weathered poles,
While shadows consume the pasture.

Vess Quinlan

Range Cow in Winter

Have you listened still on a desert hill
　　At the close of a bitter day,
When the orange sun in wispy clouds
　　Was set in a greenish haze?
In a cold white world of deepening drifts
　　That cover the land like a pall,
Then the plaintive bawl of a hungry cow
　　Is the loneliest sound of all!

Have you listened still on a desert hill
　　When the world was cold and drear,
When the tinkling bells of a herd of sheep
　　Was the nearest sound you'd hear,
And the haunting notes of a lone coyote whose
　　Evening's hunting howl
Rose wild and clear in the cold blue night,
　　And was answered by the hoot of an owl?

But when the scanty grass lies covered deep
　　By the snow that lies like a pall,
Then the plaintive bawl of a hungry cow
　　Is the loneliest sound of all!

Vern Mortensen

The Trail of an Old Timer's Memory

There's a trail that leads out to the mountains
Through the prairie dust velvety gray,
Through the canyons, the gulches, and coulees,
A trail that grows dimmer each day.
You can't make it without an old timer
To guide you and make you his guest,
For that trail is the long trail of memory—
And it leads to the heart of the West.

Now it winds through the shadows of sorrow,
Now it's warmed by the sunlight of smiles,
Now it lingers along pleasant waters,
Now it stretches o'er long, weary miles.
But it never is lonesome, deserted,
As you journey its distances vast
For it always is crowded and peopled
With dim phantom shapes of the past.

Freight wagons creaking and lurching
Leaving the old trading posts,
And Indian war parties scouting
As silent and furtive as ghosts;
Cowpunchers driving the trail herd,
The stage coach that swayed as she rolled
With her passengers, sourdough and pilgrim,
In quest of adventure and gold.

Cavalry trots through the dust clouds,
Hunter and trapper and scout,
Miner and trader and outlaw
All meet on this marvelous route
Where laughter and tears are found mingled,
Where a prince may be found in a shack,
On this trail to the days 'most forgotten,
The days that will never come back.

Robert Fletcher